D1458302

CONTENTS

1

Flossie Goes Dancing

"Now, what tights shall I wear today?" thought Flossie Teacake to herself.

Actually, she thought it aloud. Flossie liked to hear herself think. Thinking and talking were the same thing to Flossie. She often found she didn't know what she thought, until she had talked.

"I know, I'll put on my new pink Lycra ones. They haven't seen them yet."

So Flossie went to her drawers to find the tights, which was quite easy as they were sticking out, just where she'd tried to shove them in. Her drawers were the most awful mess, but that was her problem. Now that she was ten, her mother had said she had to be in charge of keeping her own room tidy. She relied on Flossie to keep it neat. If she found Flossie's room was becoming as disgusting a mess as Bella's, then the rules would have to change.

7

Flossie wished all the rules would change. Her ambition in life was to have her room as disgusting as Bella's. Well, one of her ambitions. Flossie Teacake had many ambitions in life—a lot of them to do with Bella.

Bella was Flossie's big sister, aged eighteen, and she had been allowed to give up all those domestic rules years and years ago. It wasn't fair, Flossie thought. Bella was allowed to get away with everything and anything. What Flossie feared was that when she became eighteen, if she ever did, and sometimes she believed it would never ever happen, the rules would completely change. That would be typical of her luck.

Flossie stood looking at herself in the mirror, breathing in deeply. No, she wasn't trying to look slimmer. Flossie was prepared to punch anyone who said she wasn't slim. She would agree that she was plumpish, but that was all. Bella was so slim you could hardly see her.

"But who wants to look like stupid old Bella?" asked Flossie. Then she thought for a moment.

"Me," she replied, answering her own question.

She breathed in again several more times, admir-

ing her new pink tights in the mirror. Breathing in deeply was very good for you, so Flossie knew.

"Good for your acrobats," said Flossie. "Or is it aerodynamics? Or even aerodromes. Something stupid like that." Everything that Flossie didn't understand at once was stupid. She'd seen these exercises in a book her mother had been given for Christmas.

"I do look *very* slim today," said Flossie, quite surprised. She'd only had two helpings of mint choc ice-cream last night, though she had wanted three.

"Hmm, not bad, Flos," she said to herself. "Well done, Flos."

If you're going to talk to yourself, Flossie always maintained, you might as well address yourself by your Christian name. It made talking-to-yourself conversations more friendly. Somehow.

"I hope I'm not turning into Anna Rexic. Don't want to be her. She's the slimmest girl in the whole world. I've heard people talking about her. All the same, Flos, you *are* losing weight."

Flossie got nearer the mirror, peering very hard. Then she stopped and frowned, furious at herself for forgetting.

She gave a kick at Fido who just managed to escape. He had been lying on the circular yellow rug in the middle of Flossie's bedroom floor, watching her getting dressed. It was always good fun watching Flossie get up and get dressed every morning. Better than watching television any time.

"You stupid dog," said Flossie. "Take that grin off your stupid face."

Flossie kicked her way across the room to her bed and picked up her specs from her little bedside table. She had forgotten to put them on. No wonder she had looked so slim.

"Stupid specs. Why do I have to wear them? Bella doesn't wear specs. S'not fair."

The moment Flossie put her spectacles on she decided her new pink tights were horrid. They made her look fat and she was never wearing them again, so she threw them at Fido. They landed on his head and he started barking and shaking them, thinking it was a game.

Instead, Flossie put on her purple Lycra tights. A darker colour is always more flattering for the fuller figure, Flossie thought. Then she put on her black leotard. She chose a suitable T-shirt from her selection of suitable T-shirts, all hanging out of the bottom drawer of her chest of drawers, and put it on over her leotard.

"Now, which leg warmers?" The Teacakes did have central heating, but Flossie always put on leg warmers every morning, even in summer. Especially on Saturday mornings. Saturday morning was the morning she wanted to look her very best.

To complete her wardrobe, she put on her multi-coloured leg warmers. Quite a contrast, so she thought, with her black leotard and her red T-shirt. Rather dashing.

Flossie opened her bedroom door and listened carefully on the landing. There was no noise. Bella and Fergus must already be up.

Fergus was her big brother, aged sixteen, and he played football most Saturday mornings, so he would already be downstairs, stuffing his face. There would probably be nothing left for breakfast by the time she got to the table.

Flossie very quietly opened the door to Fergus's room and peeped inside. His bedclothes were all over the floor. Yes, he was up and gone. She tiptoed to his table and carefully picked up his new sweat-bands, those woolly things which people like tennis players put on their wrists. Fergus just seemed to have his for decoration. She had never seen him wear them yet. They had some words printed on them—SPURS. That was the football team he supported.

"How stupid," thought Flossie, slowly putting them on. "They're meant to be used. Hmm, quite a good fit."

Then she grimaced. "Oh God, don't say I'm getting fat wrists now."

Flossie came down the stairs, followed by Fido, sniffing behind her.

She caught sight of herself in the hall mirror as she reached the bottom of the stairs.

"Yes, not bad, Flossie. Those wrist bands make *all* the difference. I bet nobody's ever thought of wearing them before. I could be starting a new fashion."

Flossie tried her hair in several different ways, but didn't spend too long. She always had her hair in a pony tail for dancing. Just like the professionals, when they did their professional dance practice.

"I might get spotted today," said Flossie. "Today might be the day I become HUGE . . ."

"You are huge," said Fergus, eating his way through three slices of toast. "And you talk to yourself too much. I think you look ridiculous."

"Shut up, you," said Flossie, walking into the kitchen. "Pig."

"No, now, that's enough of that, you two," said Mrs Teacake. "Just sit down, Flossie, and have your breakfast."

Flossie went to the kitchen cupboard and got out the sugar bowl and then sat down at her place. Mrs Teacake got up and took the sugar bowl away from Flossie and put it back in the cupboard.

"Oh, it's a game, is it?" said Flossie. "I see. Find the sugar bowl. Very funny. But I'm not in a mood for games. You fetch it, Fido, there's a good dog."

Fido waved his tail and looked up at Flossie adoringly. She was pouring out cornflakes while scowling and putting on her blackest look.

"Eating cornflakes is bad enough," said her mother, "as they're full of sugar, but putting more sugar on them is just ridiculous."

"Quite right, Mother," said Fergus.

"Creep," said Flossie.

"I agree with Mother," said Fergus.

"Double creep," said Flossie.

"Seriously, Flossie," said Mother, "I have told you. Sugar is your enemy."

"Oh God, not that one again," moaned Flossie. "You're always saying stupid things like that. Yesterday you said Butter is My Enemy. Then before that it was Cream is My Enemy. Seems to me everything is my enemy! You'll be saying water is my enemy next. Or fresh air is my enemy. You don't want me to have any fun in life. You're horrid to me. All of you . . ."

Mrs Teacake was quietly reading the newspaper. Mr Teacake was carefully opening his post. Fergus was busy on his fourth slice. None of them appeared to be taking any notice of Flossie. They had heard all this before.

It even looked as if Mr Teacake might be half smiling, judging by a slight tremor at the corner of his lips. Flossie watched carefully. Being ignored was one thing. But anyone who dared to laugh at Flossie would really get a mouthful. But no, Mr Teacake appeared to be amused by a letter. He leaned across and pointed it out to Mrs Teacake and they both smiled.

Flossie took the chance to pour out another helping of cornflakes while they weren't watching. That would teach them to be horrible to her.

"I saw that," said her mother, picking up Flossie's bowl and putting half the contents back in the packet.

"Cornflakes are your enemy," said Flossie, putting on a silly voice, pretending to talk like her mother.

"Quite right, dear," said her mother. "I'm glad you've got the message at last."

Flossie got down from the breakfast table, scraping her chair the way she wasn't supposed to, and went into the living room.

"May I leave the table, Mother?" said Fergus sweetly. He was just showing off.

"Triple creep," shouted Flossie.

Flossie put on a record, lay down on the floor and started some simple stretching exercises.

"Dad, you've got fifteen minutes," shouted Flossie. "You'd better be ready in time. O.K.?"

"Don't worry, my petal," said Mr Teacake.

When Mr Teacake was being jolly, he often called Flossie "petal", just as a joke. It quite amused Flossie as well. Slowly, her moany face slid away as she did her exercises.

"Come here, Flossie Teacake," said Fergus. He was standing in the middle of the living room, watching her. "What have you got on your wrists, eh?"

"Shurrup," said Flossie. "Can't you see I'm busy?"

"Flossie, if they're what I think they are, you are for it . . ."

"Get lost," said Flossie. "Mum, he's ruining my exercises . . ."

"Fergus, leave her alone while she's busy," said Mother from the kitchen, still reading the newspaper.

"Mum, she's pinched some of my things . . ."

17

"What things?" asked Flossie, all innocent.

"On your wrists, dum dum," said Fergus. "They belong to me."

"How can my wrists belong to you? Don't be stupid."

"I mean those wrist bands. They're my Spurs wrist bands."

"What are you on about?" said Flossie. "They're bandages. I hurt my wrists yesterday in gym at school. Miss Button said I had to wear these special bandages all weekend. So there. And get out of the way. Mum, tell him. Fergus, please keep out of the way."

"Fergus, do leave her alone."

Flossie stood up and did some of her very quickest dancing steps, her best routines, going so quickly that Fergus couldn't see if there were any words written on her wrist bands, or even if they were wrist bands. Perhaps after all they were bandages.

"You can't dance anyway," said Fergus. "You're just a lump. You'll never make a dancer in a million years."

"You can't annoy me," said Flossie. "I don't care what you say. Ha ha ha."

But she was annoyed. Although she had decided to teach herself not to be upset when Fergus said cruel things to her, it was very hard. Luckily, her mother came in and told Fergus that if he was going to play football, he'd better hurry up and get ready.

"And you can't play football," said Flossie. "You're useless at it. Just as useless as Spurs . . ."

Fergus tried to trip her up as he went out of the door, but he didn't manage it.

Flossie, for all her un-thinness, could be quite quick, when she wanted to.

In the car, on the way to her dancing class in Covent Garden, Flossie sat with her father at the front. It was just the two of them. Going to Covent Garden had become their new Saturday morning ritual. Dad dropped her at the Grapefruit Studios, in time for her dance lesson, while he went off by himself to do his own thing.

"You know, Flos," said her father, "I can't decide who has the more exciting Saturday morning. Me or you. Do you know, last week I nearly bought a Penny Black. Not a good one, of course. Very tatty and dirty."

"Why don't you buy a Penny White, then?" said Flossie. "Who wants a dirty old Penny Black."

Flossie could never understand what her father saw in stamps. It seemed a really boring hobby to her. Really stupid. Imagine, collecting little scraps of old paper. Even babies in the Infants Class wouldn't do that. But her father did drive her every week to Covent Garden, which was much easier than the bus, so Flossie tried her hardest to be polite and interested in his hobby.

"How's the splits coming on, Flossie?" asked her father.

"I'm almost half way there," said Flossie.

"Oh, that's good," said Mr Teacake, humming to himself.

Mr Teacake could never understand what Flossie saw in dancing. It seemed really pointless to him. All that throwing yourself about and twisting your arms and your legs into funny positions. Babies could do that sort of thing so much easier than large-ish ten-year-olds.

But Flossie did like going to Covent Garden with him every week, and that gave him a good excuse to go round the stamp shops. Around Covent Garden there are the best stamp shops in the whole world. Very convenient for Mr Teacake. So he always tried his hardest to be polite and interested in Flossie's hobby.

The Grapefruit Dance Studios are in a large old-fashioned-looking warehouse building in Covent Garden. At least it looks old-fashioned from the outside, being a dark building up a narrow alleyway, but inside it is all brightness and flashing lights and loud music.

Once through the front door, past rows of dancing clothes for sale, Flossie was swept along by a stream of young people wearing the latest dance fashions and looking terribly fit and very important. All of them gave the impression that they were not just on the way to a rather hot and sweaty bout of physical exercise but on the way to being DISCOVERED.

That was what Flossie liked most of all about going to the Grapefruit Studios. She was positive she would be the next person in the world to be DIS-COVERED. Surely, her name must come up soon. She had had it down for absolutely ages. For as long as she could remember, Flossie had been waiting. And not very patiently either.

Flossie made her way to the basement studios as quickly as possible, walking on the tippy tips of her toes, the way the best dancers always walk, elegantly and effortlessly, without appearing to hurry. This was quite hard to do, Flossie being only ten, a bit small and un-thin, and because she was carrying a large Adidas sports bag belonging to Fergus (he didn't know about that either). Inside, she had a change of leotard, dancing shoes, pink tights, a spare T-shirt, some Elastoplast and other articles of clothing she had thought about wearing in the first place but had decided to bring with her, just in case.

"If one is going to be Discovered," thought Flossie, "one has to be Prepared."

She went quickly to the changing room and got ready. This did not take long as she had already decided she was wearing her best dancing clothes. All she took off was her school coat which her mother had *forced* her to wear, being really stupid, saying she might catch cold when she came out. Flossie just hoped nobody had seen her arriving in it. "I bet

Rudolf Nureyev doesn't have to wear his school coat when he goes to dancing practice."

Flossie's class was called funky disco dancing, or, as Mr Teacake insisted on calling it, dunky fisco dancing. It was always held in a basement room. This was the only thing Flossie disliked about her dancing practice. Even in the winter time, it got very hot and very sticky. In that hour's practice every week, Flossie was convinced she lost hundreds of pounds. That was why she *had* to eat extra sugar and sweets, just to make up for the enormous weight and energy loss.

"Flossie, can you come out to the front and help me demonstrate this new exercise, please."

It was Lizzie talking, the dancing teacher in charge of the class. Flossie was very pleased to be picked out, but she was a bit nervous about standing in front of the whole group. She liked Lizzie, who was very kind and nice and not rude and cruel, like some people Flossie could mention.

It was a mixed age class. In fact Flossie was almost the youngest dancer. Most of them were about thirteen or fourteen, boys as well as girls, though mostly girls. Some considered themselves quite grown up and rather looked down on Flossie. She was quite used to that. She had had to put up with Fergus and Bella all her life so far. She knew what to expect from stupid teenagers.

There were two girls in particular, only about a year older than Flossie, who were always trying to boss her around. They were Cindy and Tracey. They couldn't really dance any better than Flossie, but they thought they could and they were always telling Flossie that she'd got the steps wrong.

Flossie helped Lizzie by fetching her Boogie Box —which is what Lizzie called her record-player machine: a large silvery, shiny music player, the sort Flossie would have liked to carry around everywhere with her, but her parents had definitely put their feet down about that.

Lizzie switched it on and the latest disco tune immediately boomed round the studio. She demonstrated some new steps and the whole class started throwing themselves around, especially Flossie.

Very soon, Flossie was rather out of breath, but as she was still at the front, near Lizzie, she had to keep going, puff-puffing away.

"Now," said Lizzie. "I haven't thought of the best way to finish that dance. Any ideas? Flossie, what do you think?"

"How about a split?" suggested Flossie.

"Don't you mean *splits*?" said Lizzie.

Everyone laughed, especially Cindy and Tracey. They were jealous that they hadn't been asked by Lizzie to come to the front of the class.

"When you do it with two legs," explained Flossie, "then it's called splits. But with one leg, it's just a split. I am practising on two legs, so I might be able to do both splits by this time next week . . ."

Everyone started laughing again, really loudly this time. Lizzie waved to them to be quiet and then she turned the music off, showing them it was the end of the class.

"Well, I thought that was a jolly good idea, Flossie," said Lizzie. "Well done. Thanks for helping."

Flossie turned away, fed up with the dancing class, especially the other girls in it. It wasn't fair. She could see in the long mirrors, with her own eyes, how good she really was, but *they* didn't realize . . .

"Oh, Flossie, could you go back and give out this notice for me, please," said Lizzie. "I forgot to tell the class."

Flossie was sitting in the dressing room. She had been first out, not wanting to listen to the comments of people like Cindy and Tracey. Lizzie, as usual, was in a mad rush as she ran off to her next class at another dance studio.

Flossie decided not to go back into the studio. She would wait for them all to join her in the dressing room. She was too tired anyway. Very slowly, she took off her dancing shoes and put on her street shoes and then her boring school coat and slowly went upstairs to wait for her father.

She was in the car, being driven home, when she remembered the notice Lizzie had given her. She looked at it quickly. It said that there would be no funky disco lesson next week as Lizzie would be away, but the class would resume the week after. Lizzie was very often away these days, now that she was becoming well known as a dancing teacher.

"What's that, Flossie?" asked her father.

"Oh, nothing," said Flossie. "Just an old scrap of paper. Rubbish, really."

"That's what you say about my stamps," said her father.

"Oh, it's not as boring as *that*," said Flossie. "But almost."

And with that, Flossie tore up the notice. Very slowly, she dropped it, piece by piece, on the floor of the car when her father wasn't looking . . .

The next Saturday morning, Flossie was awake rather later than usual. She got her dancing clothes ready and came out on to the top landing, checking if Bella and Fergus were already up. There was not a sound from their bedrooms.

She went first to Fergus's room, but she didn't open the door, just stood for a few moments and listened. Then she went to Bella's room. On her door was a notice.

"Keep Out, Guard Dogs, Dangerous, No Admittance and This Means You, Flossie."

"Bella is a pig," said Flossie. "Trust her to be horrible."

Flossie waited for some time, her ear to the key-hole, just in case there should be anyone inside. She pushed the door open carefully and stepped back, expecting there might be a trap, perhaps a bucket of water ready to fall on her head. That was the sort of rotten trick Bella might play on her.

Then she slowly went into Bella's room. It was even more chaotic than it had been the last time she was in it. Bella must have been to more jumble sales and bought more old clothes, old carpets, busts, skeletons, broken chairs, legs, skulls, notices, mirrors, plates, bottles. She could see an old bath chair, the sort invalids used to have, which she had never noticed before, and what looked like the remains of a motorbike and sidecar. How on earth had Bella got it up the stairs and into her room without her father seeing?

"I'm telling on that Bella," said Flossie. "I'm telling Dad straight away. There's oil all over the floor. I can see where it's been dripping."

Then Flossie gave a little jump.

"Or is it blood!"

She stood for a while, wondering what to do, then she realized it was only red paint on an old jagged piece of mirror.

"No, I won't tell anyone," said Flossie to herself. "It might come in useful, if ever Bella tells on me . . ."

Flossie's eyes and ears eventually became used to the gloom. She carefully climbed over all the piles of clothes and furniture and managed to fight her way to the far corner of Bella's room. It was still there, the pink-painted, curly-topped, hat stand. And hanging from it was the Magic Fur Coat.

Flossie listened again. There were various little creaks and noises coming from inside the room as objects and parcels and ornaments, which Flossie had disturbed as she clambered over them, returned to their normal shape. But there were no human noises, either inside or outside the room. She was alone.

Flossie took down the huge fur coat. It seemed to dwarf her completely. It was still as black and shiny as ever and she imagined she could see the shapes of animals lurking inside the fur.

"Oh, please let it still work," said Flossie, closing her eyes.

She crept into the coat, holding her breath, and very slowly put her hands out, feeling for the buttons. Then she started to do them up, one by one. She turned round and round inside the coat, completely lost from sight, wishing and wishing with all her might that the magic would work once again.

"Oh, *please* let me be eighteen. I want to be eighteen now, just like Bella, more than anything else in the whole world . . ."

As she did up the last button, she opened her eyes and felt a strange sensation in her body. She seemed to be suddenly growing and growing and growing. The fur coat was now fitting her perfectly, yet it hadn't changed at all. It was Flossie who had changed. She had miraculously been transformed into an eighteen-year-old, exactly the same age as her big sister Bella, the age she had always wanted to be.

Flossie had jumped forward in time by exactly eight years and had become a real teenager. But inside her physically grown-up body there was still the same ten-year-old Flossie, with the same ten-year-old's thoughts and feelings.

"Hurray," she said, clapping her hands. Then she did a strange thing. She took the coat off again.

Mr Teacake was looking for a parking place. Every Saturday morning he moaned and groaned about trying to find a parking place. One Saturday morning he had been fined ten pounds and had vowed never to come again, but he always did. He *had* to come, he said, for Flossie's dancing classes.

At last he saw a free meter. Flossie jumped out and guided him into it, stopping a green Rolls Royce from getting in first.

"Thanks, Flos," said her father.

They hurried through the streets to the Grapefruit dancing class. They were rather late, having had such trouble parking.

"Here, let me carry your bag," said her father, suddenly taking it from her. "What *have* you got in it? I know you always travel with a complete change of wardrobe, but this is ridiculous. Have you put the kitchen sink in it today?"

Mr Teacake stopped and started to unzip the bag,

but Flossie quickly grabbed it from him.

"Don't open it!" Flossie had shouted a little too loudly and her father looked suspicious.

"Sorry," said Flossie. "Anyway, I can carry it myself. Lizzie's doing some really special exercises this week and we've got to bring lots of extra clothes, see."

"All the more reason for me to carry it, then," said her father.

"No, no," said Flossie. "I don't want you to get exhausted, Dad. You'll need all your strength for your stamps. I know it's pretty tiring picking up those tweezers."

They were on the steps of the Grapefruit Studios by now, so Flossie gave her father a quick kiss.

"See you in an hour," said Flossie. "Don't come too early. It could be a long lesson today . . ."

Flossie went downstairs to the changing rooms —and then straight into the lavatory where she locked the door. She didn't want other people to see what was inside her bag. Very quickly, she got out the Magic Fur Coat.

33

"Will it still work in here?" she wondered to herself.

In the past, she had always put on the Magic Fur Coat inside Bella's bedroom. She was so excited she did it up much quicker than usual, buttoning all the buttons in one movement, but remembering to wish that she could be eighteen—now. And it worked! She had become Floz, an elegant and beautiful eighteen-year-old. To her amazement, she was dressed underneath the fur coat in the same sort of dancing clothes that Lizzie usually wore.

"That's lucky," said Floz. "I couldn't have carried any other clothes with me this week."

"Heh, Cindy," said a voice which sounded very much like Tracey's. "There's some loony in the lav talking to herself. Come and listen."

Floz had not realized she had been talking to herself. It was something she had often done, oh, when she was very much younger. She stood still and kept very quiet, hoping they would go away, but outside the lavatory door she could hear some very heavy breathing.

Suddenly, she opened the door quickly and sent Cindy and Tracey flying across the floor.

"If *you* two are in my class today, then you'd better hurry up," said Floz, striding across the changing room, down the corridor and into the dance studio. When you are eighteen, you do take terribly long strides, compared with little twelve-year-olds like Cindy and Tracey.

"Lizzie is not here today," said Floz, standing in front of the class, looking very severe. "So she has asked me to take charge, just for this class. I should really be on Top of the Pops, teaching them how to dance, but I decided to help you lot instead. By the look of some of you, you could do with a great deal of help."

Floz was looking straight at Cindy and Tracey. They were at the back of the room, still puzzled by what was going on.

"Right, first of all, we'll begin with the splits. You two at the back! Stop hiding there, girls, and come out here and show us all how good you are."

Tracey and Cindy managed to get their legs into a sort of V shape, but neither could manage a proper set of splits, or even a good single split.

"Isn't there a little girl called Flossie here today?" asked Floz. "Has anyone seen her? Lizzie's told me she's terribly good for her age. Well, never mind. We'll start with some easy-peasy stretching exercises, just to warm you all up."

Floz demonstrated a few bending exercises, still wearing her fur coat, which they all copied. Then she went to the cupboard where Lizzie kept her Boogie Box and got it out. She told them she wanted to see them doing the new dance steps which Lizzie had taught them last week.

"Only," said Floz, switching on the music, "I want you to do it at double speed."

They were soon all absolutely exhausted while Floz stood there, watching them and smiling.

"Ain't you doing any exercises, Miss?" said Cindy, when Floz at last told them they could stop.

"She can't," whispered Tracey, nudging Cindy. "Not with that flea-bitten fur coat on."

They both giggled, but Floz pretended not to notice.

"I am under contract, you see," explained Floz,

putting on her best film star voice. "My agent does not allow me to dance with amateurs, only with *real* dancers. I've promised the Royal Opera House, Wayne Sleep, Bob Fosse, Margot Fonteyn and The Bolshy Theatre to keep their secrets. I've taught them everything they know."

Tracey and Cindy were still giggling. Their new teacher did appear very smart and elegant and professional, but could she really dance? That fur coat did seem a strange thing to wear, they thought, for a dance teacher.

"My coat eez from my Russian grandmother," said Floz. "All zee best dancers in Russia have a coat like zeez."

Suddenly Floz started to unbutton it, letting it hang open on the top button, to reveal a brilliantly striped leotard, a star-studded T-shirt and leg warmers made of real fur. She then proceeded to go into the most amazing dance routine any of them had ever seen, her fur coat flying round her like a bull fighter's cloak.

When you are eighteen, and have been to dance lessons all your life, and you are tall and very slender and not at all plump and you don't wear spectacles and you have long very black hair, then naturally you know all there is to know about dancing.

When Floz finally finished, the whole class broke into loud cheers and tremendous clapping.

"Now I've got a surprise for you," said Floz. "It's far too hot in here, don't you agree?"

They all shouted, "Yes." Floz, of course, in her fur coat, felt it most of all.

"Let's go outside instead," said Floz. "We'll let the whole of London see just what brilliant dancers you all are. Cindy, you can carry the Boogie Box. Follow me. Let's go . . ."

First of all, they went out into the Covent Garden Piazza, Floz leading them like the Pied Piper of Hamelin. They danced through the shoppers and tourists in a line, doing their best to copy every movement that Floz made.

There were some clowns performing in front of the big church and Floz gave them a cheery wave as her troupe danced round and round them. All the children in the class waved shyly to the clowns, except Cindy and Tracey. They gave a rather cheeky wave.

"Gerroff," said the chief clown very grumpily. "This is our pitch."

"Oh, you're playing football, are you?" said Floz. "I didn't think you were clowns. Not funny enough for clowns. You want to get some wrist bands. Then you'll play better football. Bye-ee."

Floz then led her class through the market stalls, threading their way in and out amongst the crowds. Cindy was finding it hard to keep up as she was still carrying the Boogie Box. At the end of the stalls they came to a little open area where Floz told Cindy she could put down the music box for a while and have a rest.

"Now we'll do our *best* dancing," said Floz. "Those steps we learned last week. All line up. Cindy, music please . . ."

A large crowd quickly gathered to watch Floz and her dancing class and very soon the crowd were clapping in time to the music. Some even started cheering. Floz was the best dancer, of course, being the teacher, but the others did very well. Even Cindy and Tracey.

One little boy decided to throw some pennies, and others followed.

Floz went to the Boogie Box, pressed a button, and on came *Money, Money, Money*, that tune by ABBA. When the crowd heard this, even more money poured in.

At the far end of the stalls, Floz could see a policewoman making her way towards them. Floz thought that perhaps she was coming to join in, or even to ask for help in organizing the Police Ball.

"Stop this at once!" said the policewoman, standing right in front of Floz.

"It's a fair cop," said Floz, stopping the music. The crowd all laughed at Floz's joke.

"Have you got a licence?" said the policewoman.

"I'm too young to drive a car," said Floz. "My dad does the driving."

"I don't mean that sort of licence," said the policewoman.

"Oh, a dog licence," said Floz. "Sorry. My dog doesn't drive either."

"I mean a permit for busking in a public place for financial reward."

"Oh, I see, Officer," said Floz. "But we're doing it

for fun. We didn't ask for the money. Here, you can have it all. Give it to the Home for Retired Police-women. We're a proper dance class, you know. Well, must keep dancin' . . ."

Floz turned and led her dancing class off through the crowds. The policewoman smiled and put away her notebook.

The dancers then went down a side street, Floz still leading the way, with Tracey this time carrying the Boogie Box.

"We need a proper stage to perform on," said Floz. "Some big square where thousands of people can watch us. I know! Follow me."

When they came to the edge of Trafalgar Square the traffic was so busy they couldn't get across, especially as they were still in line, doing all their very clever and intricate dance steps.

Floz stopped at the kerb, beside a long row of red double-decker buses. There was only a little gap between each one, too narrow for even someone as thin and slender as Floz to squeeze through. She might just manage, but she knew Cindy and Tracey would never do it.

"Wait here, class," said Floz. "I'll handle this performance."

Floz had noticed a large tree at each corner of the square. She did a couple of hand-stands on the pavement, then a few cartwheels and splits, just to warm up, then she dashed between the buses and headed for the nearest tree. She climbed up it so quickly she almost seemed to fly.

When you're eighteen and run a dance class and you are an expert on all things acrobatic, not to mention aerobic, you can easily do all sorts of clever tricks.

"Are you watching, class?" shouted Floz from the top of the tree. "The next bit is more difficult."

With one leap, Floz jumped from an overhanging branch of the tree right on to the roof of one of the double-decker buses.

"Now, class!" shouted Floz. "When you dance at the London Palladium, you often have to perform on a revolving stage. So this is very good practice. Watch me terribly carefully."

Floz then started dancing along the line of London buses, jumping from one roof to another. They were all so close it was quite easy. Sometimes she did a cartwheel from one to another, just to show off.

The class followed her along the pavement, Tracey turning up the music to top volume, so that Floz could hear it. They all clapped in time, feeling very proud of their teacher. People all over Trafalgar Square stopped to watch Floz's exhibition. Even Nelson seemed to turn to admire her (using his good eye, of course).

When Floz had danced and jumped her way along the roofs of eighteen big buses, she realized she had come to the end of the queue. The next bus was about thirty metres away. Even Floz couldn't jump that far.

Luckily, there was a lorry nearby, so she jumped on to it from the top of the bus. Ahead of the lorry was a slightly smaller one, so she jumped down again.

"Now, what shall I do?" thought Floz. "It's a bit high even for me to jump on to the road. I don't want to hurt my ankles by landing too heavily."

As she was thinking, a taxi came alongside. Very quickly, Floz leapt from the little lorry and landed lightly on the taxi.

44

Floz did a few bows and waves, then she leaned over the taxi roof to thank the driver for his kindness. He looked very startled to find an upside-down face suddenly grinning through his window.

Floz then jumped down on to the pavement where her class were waiting for her. They burst into three loud cheers. It was the best dancing performance they had ever seen.

"Quick, there she is! She's over there!"

Floz looked round to see where the shouts had come from. She thought it might be one of the bus drivers, perhaps an inspector come to ask her for her ticket. It was a man with what looked like a glass eye round his neck, carrying a clipboard.

"Miss, Miss," he shouted, running towards her. "Stop!"

Floz stared at him, then turned round, wondering if perhaps he was talking to someone behind her back, but he rushed right up to her and grabbed her by the shoulder.

"I've got her," he yelled towards a group of about eight people who were standing in the middle of

Trafalgar Square, by the fountain. "Hurry up! Quick."

"What's going on?" said Floz.

"You were marvellous, darling, absolutely super, just what we wanted," said the man. "We're doing a Day in the Life of Trafalgar Square for London Weekend Television—and you are the first lovely thing that's happened to us all day."

"What?" said Floz.

Even though she was eighteen, a grown-up woman of the world, dance teacher extraordinary, Floz could sometimes be a bit slow on the uptake.

"We've got you on a long shot, jumping on the buses. God, it was amazing. Magic, absolute magic. You're a natural, my dear. Now we need a few close-ups. Don't move. Just stand there . . ."

Floz stood on the pavement, with the television director practically putting her arm in a lock so she couldn't move away, while eight people huffed and puffed across the road, carting tripods, lights, sound equipment and a camera.

"Miss, what's going on?" asked Cindy.

"Oh, just another television company," said Floz. "They're always wanting me to appear. Now, if you're all *very* good, you can be on with me. You could be Discovered. As well as me. Tracey, do you think my hair's O.K., hmm?"

When the camera crew had set up their equipment on the pavement, Floz was asked to do a few steps, to limber up on the pavement, as if she was about to jump on the buses. She had to do it several times. Firstly some passers-by got in the way. Then there was a very noisy lorry. Then the sun went in.

"Sorry, Rog," said the camera-man, after the fourth attempt. "Now we've got a hair in the gate."

"What's that mean?" asked Tracey.

"Oh, it's a TV term," said Floz, offhand. "They keep all sorts of animals in those cameras these days. It's the modern method. A rabbit or a hare must have got loose, I s'pose."

Roger, the director, smiled. "It just means, girls, that there's a bit of dirt on the lens of the camera. Won't be a minute."

"I *knew* that," said Floz. "Just kidding."

"Of course you were, my dear," said Roger. This time Floz did her steps without anything going wrong.

"Right, that was brill, absolutely brill. Now all I

47

want is a little interview with you. You don't mind, do you? There will be a payment, of course. By the way, I don't know your name . . ."

At last, Floz really was going to be Discovered. Not just dancing on TV, but talking on TV. And getting paid for it . . .

Roger arranged Floz on a suitable spot on the pavement, in a good position, so the light was on her, with her dancing class gathered round and behind her the mighty roar of the London buses. At Floz's feet, kneeling on the pavement, crouched a sound man, holding his microphone almost up Floz's nose, ready to catch every word which Floz might speak and record it for posterity.

Just as the clapper board came down, and the director shouted "Action", a taxi screeched to a halt and stopped quite near Floz and the little group of television people.

Inside the cab was a lady passenger. She was wearing dancer's clothes and holding a sporting bag on her knee. She seemed rather familiar to Floz. It took her only a few seconds to realize who it was. It was Lizzie. She was on her way to another of her dancing classes.

"Why, that's my class!" shouted Lizzie, opening the window. "What on earth are you all doing here? Were you the person jumping on the buses . . . ?"

"Quick," said Floz. "Come on, class. We've got to get going."

Floz grabbed Tracey and Cindy by the hand and pulled them off through the crowd which had gathered round to watch the filming. All the others in the class immediately followed.

Floz led them away as quickly as she could. There was lots of shouting behind her and this time she was sure a policeman had seen what was going on and had come to question her.

Lizzie's taxi moved on, heading in the direction of Covent Garden. In the back seat, Lizzie rubbed her eyes. Had she imagined that strange scene in Trafalgar Square?

Meanwhile, Floz was running with her class in the direction of the Strand, looking for a quiet place to hide . . .

Mr Teacake was examining a Penny Red. It wasn't a very good one, just two margins and rather scruffy, but it was only fifty p. He had been looking for this particular one for a long time because the letters at the top of the stamp read F.T. Perfect.

He was standing inside Stanley Gibbons, the world's greatest stamp shop. As usual, the shop was busy, but very quiet. Stamp collectors, when examining their treasures, don't make a lot of noise.

Suddenly, the huge glass doors opened and into the stamp shop came a long line of children wearing strange clothes. One of them was carrying a large tape recorder.

"This will do," said Floz. "We'll just wait here a few moments. Down on the floor, please. We'll do some quiet stretching exercises."

"Where's this place?" asked Cindy.

"It could be the front of a new theatre, with that huge glass window," said Floz. "I think I saw 'Cats' here. It might even be the National Theatre. Right, now we'll have some music please, Tracey."

And they started their dancing once again, stepping round and over all the stamp counters, jumping piles of albums, up and down the open staircase. Floz did one particularly huge leap—and landed right beside her father.

"What's going on?" said her father. "Don't I know you?"

"Never seen you in my life before," said Floz.

From a little room, the manager came out to discover what all the noise was about.

"After me, class," shouted Floz. "This is just a boring stamp shop. We'll do our audition for 'Starlight Express' some other time. Right, I think it's now time to return to the studio . . ."

Back at the Grapefruit Studios, Floz dismissed her class and put the Boogie Box away in the locker where Lizzie always kept it.

"Can we do that dance again next week, Miss?" said Tracey and Cindy together as they left the studio. "It was really good."

"I'm not sure," said Floz. "I've got some more television work next week. But I think Lizzie will be back to look after you. Bye-ee."

Floz waited till they had all changed and left the dressing room, then she went into the lavatory and took off her Magic Fur Coat. Immediately, eighteen-year-old Floz turned back into Flossie, only ten.

Flossie packed the fur coat into her bag and then went upstairs to wait dutifully for her father.

In the car, on the way home, Mr Teacake was telling Flossie about a very funny thing which had happened to him when he was looking at stamps.

"These odd people suddenly burst into the shop. I think they thought it was a theatre. Anyway, they started doing an audition."

"Who were they?" asked Flossie.

"Well, they looked like a troupe of dancers, probably from one of those acting schools. They were quite good, actually."

"I'd like to go to acting school," said Flossie. "When I'm older, of course."

"You have to be *very* good," said her father. "It's very hard to get in."

"Perhaps when I'm older," said Flossie, "I *will* be good."

Mr Teacake noticed a strange look on Flossie's face. Was she wistful, or perhaps worried about her dancing?

Maybe, he thought, she has had a very tiring

morning. After all, she is one of the youngest in the funky disco class.

"Never mind," said her father. "I've got a present for you."

And he passed her a Penny Red stamp, mounted in a little plastic envelope.

"See, it has your initials on. FT—Flossie Tea-cake. I knew you'd like that."

"Thanks, Dad," said Flossie. "But I still prefer dancing to stamps . . ."

2

Flossie and the Boutique

"Mum, do I have to?" said Flossie, standing at the front door.

Her mother was in the kitchen, giving instructions to Fergus on what she wanted him to do, how much to pay the milkman, what to say if Mrs Onions from next door called, how many loaves to get from the baker. Fergus was nodding his head, but not listening properly.

"Right, is that clear, then?" said Mrs Teacake. "And take your feet off the table, Fergus. Do I have to tell you one more time?"

She went through all the instructions again. You might have thought Mrs Teacake was going off on safari for months and months, not just out for the morning with Flossie.

"Mum, hurry up," shouted Flossie from the front door. "I'm bored of waiting."

"Bored *with* waiting," said her mother, still in the kitchen.

"I don't want *you* to come anyway," said Flossie. "I could do it all by myself. I don't need you. Right, I'm counting to three, then I'm going on my own."

Mrs Teacake did always take a long time getting ready to go out, but then she had a lot of things to do. She had taken the morning off work, especially for Flossie's sake, but she still had the house to run and meals to make and everything to organize.

"Mum, did you hear?" Flossie shouted down the hall.

She put on her best fed-up face and slouched against the wall, looking moody, the way she had seen teenagers look at street corners.

"Coming, Flossie," said her mother, gaily. "And please don't put your elbow on that hall shelf. You know it's not safe."

Flossie looked round in surprise. She hadn't realized she had put her elbow on the hall shelf. It just seemed to have happened, as she was practising her best slouch. Yet her mother couldn't possibly have seen her.

"She must be a witch," thought Flossie. "I wish

we could go shopping on her broom instead of the stupid old bus. And as for this stupid old shelf, it's stupid as well. Everything in this stupid old house is stupid."

"What did you say, dear?" said her mother, coming into the hall at last and putting on her hat and coat.

"Nothing," said Flossie, grumpily. "No point in saying nothing in this house. Nobody listens to nothing I say."

"Double negative means affirmative," said Fergus, going up the stairs. "Just off to do revision, Mum."

Flossie could see that he was carrying a pop music newspaper under his arm. He wasn't going to revise at all. What a liar.

"Oh, Mum, do we have to go?" said Flossie.

"Of course we do, dear. It's school again tomorrow and you've got no shoes."

"I'll go in my bare feet," said Flossie.

"Don't be silly, Flossie."

"Bella does," said Flossie. "I've seen her. In our street. Both feet bare. You don't call her silly."

"She's eighteen, Flossie. If she wants to ruin her

feet that's her fault. Until you are eighteen, you are my concern. Now put your coat on properly. It's cold outside."

"It's not fair," said Flossie. "Anway, I don't feel very well."

"The fresh air will make you feel much better."

"I hate fresh air," said Flossie.

"Yes, but fresh air loves you," said Mother.

"And I've got a sore foot."

"All the more reason to get new shoes."

"Sometimes, Mum," said Flossie, "you can be a right pain."

Mrs Teacake took Flossie's hand and together they went out of the front door. Flossie limped at first, putting it on, but then soon forgot as they turned the corner and headed for the bus stop.

Mrs Teacake smiled as she thought of all those times when Flossie was really little, about four or five, and had just started the Nursery Class, and used to make up excuses for not going to school. There was the time Flossie said she couldn't go as her hand had got stuck in her pocket. Then another time she said she had to stay at home to watch the kitchen clock and make sure it was working. Mrs Teacake was still smiling when they got on the bus.

It was only a few stops to the High Street and Flossie
had brightened up by the time they reached it.

One of the things Flossie really liked doing in life
was shopping. She could gaze in windows for hours,
imagining all the lovely dresses she would buy, all the
latest skirts, the crazy tops, the amazing tights, the
fantastic shoes. If only she was allowed to.

"It's not fair," said Flossie. "Bella can buy all her
clothes on her own, but I can't. Horrible."

"Bella doesn't buy *any* clothes. She gets them all
from jumbles or from skips."

"You wouldn't let me do that either. You're really
mean, you are. I wish I was eighteen."

"You will be, soon enough," said her mother.

"Oh yeh, I'll probably be an Old Age Pensioner by
the time I reach eighteen," said Flossie. "Then it will
be too late to buy proper clothes. I won't want them
any more. I'll just sit at home all day, knitting or
watching *Coronation Street*."

"Those look nice, Flossie," said Mrs Teacake,
stopping and pointing to a pair of shiny patent

leather shoes in the window of Saxone.

"Yucky," said Flossie, putting out her tongue at what she thought was a dummy in the window. The dummy immediately put out its tongue. It was a salesgirl, arranging the window.

"Yes, perhaps they are a bit shiny," said Mrs Teacake. "They'd never stay like that. You're so hard on shoes, Flossie."

"It's you that's hard on me. Everyone's hard on me."

"Now don't start that again," said Mrs Teacake. "I don't like shopping at all. I want this over with as quickly as possible."

"If we're quick, can I have a milk shake at McDonalds?" said Flossie, putting on her charming smile.

"We'll see," said Mrs Teacake.

Flossie hated people who said, "We'll see". She also hated it when you asked people how long to go and they replied "Soon". All those sorts of people were really stupid, according to Flossie.

"Heh, Mum, those look O.K.," said Flossie. "And they're not shiny."

They had been in four shops already, without any success. Either Flossie refused point-blank even to try them on, or the shop didn't have the right size in shoes that they both agreed might just be possible for school.

Mrs Teacake came across to look in the window of a rather old-fashioned shop where Flossie was pointing.

"Those ones in the far corner. At the back. They're not very expensive either. I think they're in a sale."

"I can't see the ones you mean," said Mrs Teacake. "I'd better put my specs on."

"They look my size," said Flossie. "There's a notice on them. I think it says they're in a style called Etto."

"Etto style?" said Mrs Teacake.

"Oh, that's very good," said Flossie quickly. "Everyone has them at school. Miss Button says they're the best shoes you can have for school. Always go for Etto. I heard her say it."

Mrs Teacake was rather short-sighted, though she pretended she wasn't. She feared that perhaps Flossie had inherited her poor eyesight, but she always

said that Flossie's eyes would be perfect when she was Bella's age, by which time she wouldn't have to wear specs ever again. So she told Flossie. Flossie wasn't so sure.

"Come on, Mum, let's go in."

A very old woman was serving, pulling down box after box for a mother and her very tall daughter who were sitting on a little bench, surrounded by piles of shoes. They had obviously been there a long time.

"Yes, Madam," said the assistant, very wearily, turning to Mrs Teacake. The shop was very dusty and untidy. There was a strong smell of plastic and shoe polish mixed with old cardboard.

"I want some shoes for my daughter," said Mrs Teacake. "School shoes. Good, solid, sensible sort of school shoes, nothing extreme."

"We've seen a pair in the window," said Flossie helpfully. "In the Etto style. That's what I want."

"What exactly do you mean?" said the woman with a sigh. It looked as if she now had even more customers who didn't know their own mind, or their own language.

"I'll show you," said Flossie, going over towards the window with the assistant.

Mrs Teacake took a seat while the assistant got the shoes out of the window and showed them to Flossie.

"That's them," said Flossie, very pleased.

"They look a bit big for you, dear, but I'll see what I've got in stock."

She put the shoes back in the window and went to the rear of the shop, disappearing behind a curtain. There was a lot of heavy sighing and moaning and the sound of boxes falling down, possibly on her head.

"You are clever, Flossie," said Mrs Teacake. "Imagine you seeing the shoes that Miss Button had recommended."

The elderly assistant returned at last. She was carrying a new white box which she began to open carefully for Mrs Teacake to inspect.

"Apparently," said Mrs Teacake, "these shoes are recommended for school wear."

"I don't know what the world's coming to, I'm sure," said the assistant, unwrapping the shoes. "Imagine a school recommending stiletto heels."

"Stiletto heels!" Mrs Teacake turned on Flossie. "What are you playing at? So this is what you meant by 'Style Etto' fashions. You can't even read properly. Come along. We're going. I'm very sorry about this."

Mrs Teacake grabbed Flossie's hand and pulled her rather roughly out of the shop. Flossie went on muttering that it wasn't fair.

"Why can't ten-year-olds wear high-heeled shoes . . ."

As they were heading back along the High Street, Flossie noticed a new shop on the other side, one she had never seen before. It must have opened in the last few weeks.

"Come on, child, don't dawdle," said her mother. "I've had enough of this nonsense."

Mrs Teacake had decided that what Flossie was going to get was a pair of dark blue Clark's shoes, with flat heels and good strong soles. She had seen them in Saxone, but had not mentioned them to Flossie at first, thinking they might be able to get an equally sensible pair, but perhaps in a brighter colour or a smarter design, something which Flossie might deign to wear. Now she didn't care what Flossie thought. It had all got beyond a joke.

"To think I gave up a morning's work to trail round the shops with you."

"What about my milk shake?" said Flossie. "You promised."

"Certainly not."

From across the road Flossie could distinctly hear the sound of loud pop music and see lights flashing inside the new shop.

Flash Boutique! Fashions for the Fashionable Miss!

There seemed to be shoes in the windows, as well as all sorts of wonderful clothes.

"Oh, Mum," pleaded Flossie. "Please. Just one look in the window. That's all. Don't be mean. I promise not to moan any more. If only I can just *look*, that's all."

Mrs Teacake thought for a moment. She certainly was not stopping for a milk shake, not now, but a few more seconds, looking at one final shop, well, she might just allow Flossie that. So they both went across.

"What a horrible noise," said Mrs Teacake. "How

can anybody possibly shop with that row going on? And all those lights. It's a nightmare."

In the window, Flossie suddenly spotted a pair of pink suede boots. They had flat heels, nothing silly, and were ankle length, with the tops turned slightly over, the sort of boots Robin Hood might have worn for best.

"Oh, no, that's just what I've always wanted," shouted Flossie. "And they're size 3 as well. My size. Oh, it's not fair."

Flossie turned to look at her mother, but she was deliberately staring down the street, looking at her watch.

"Ten more seconds," said Mrs Teacake. "That's all."

Flossie knew now there was no longer any point in asking. Life really was unfair. Everybody was always horrible to her. She felt near to tears.

She gave one final, lingering glance at the window, about to start crying, when her face very slowly began to change. She had seen something on the door of the shop which had instantly changed her mood . . .

Flossie and Mrs Teacake went into Saxone, hand in hand. Flossie was even skipping as she went, a sure sign that she was happy.

"Sorry I've been so rotten, Mum," said Flossie. "I couldn't help it."

"I should think so."

"Those Clark's shoes will be all right," said Flossie. "They were really the ones Miss Button said we should wear. The high heels were just a joke, Mum."

"I forgive you, then," said Mrs Teacake.

Very quickly, Mrs Teacake bought the sensible Clark's shoes. Flossie put them straight on and pronounced them a perfect fit.

Mrs Teacake was so pleased that she said they might, after all, just have time for a milk shake.

As they sat in McDonald's, Mrs Teacake thought how strange it was that Flossie's mood had suddenly changed, for no apparent reason. She was a funny little girl.

"Would you like a hamburger, Flossie? It will save me making you lunch at home."

"If you can afford it, Mum," said Flossie.

"Thank goodness we didn't go into that nasty Flash Boutique," said Mrs Teacake. "It looked appalling to me."

"If you say so, Mum," said Flossie, eating up her hamburger, a double one, with double chips.

It was a small notice on the door of the Flash Boutique which had changed Flossie's mood. Just eight words, but they were enough to make Flossie's little heart start beating very, very quickly.

"Wanted. Part-time Assistant. Must be over eighteen."

"Just going out to play, Mum," said Flossie.

Mrs Teacake was getting ready to go off to work for the afternoon. She had missed the morning session at the surgery where she worked as a receptionist, so she didn't want to be late.

"I'll be back by five o'clock," said Mrs Teacake. "Bella will make you something to eat if you're hungry."

"Don't worry, Mum," said Flossie. "I'm playing with Carol. Her mum said I can have tea with her."

Flossie went out of the front door with her mother. While Mrs Teacake turned one way, to go to work, Flossie turned the other, heading for Carol's house, but the moment Mrs Teacake had gone round the corner, Flossie returned home and rang the bell.

"Oh, it's you," said Fergus, very bad-tempered. He hated coming all the way downstairs to answer the front door, especially when it wasn't for him.

"Thank you, my man," said Flossie, pushing her way past him. "Forgotten something. I'll be going out again, so I won't bother you any more, Your Majesty."

Flossie ran upstairs. She waited till Fergus was safely back in his room, then she went on tiptoe to Bella's room. She knew that Bella had gone out for the day with her friends. She was always out somewhere.

The Magic Fur Coat was in its place on the coat stand, exactly as Flossie had left it there last time. It was strange that Bella never wore it, but then she had so many things in her room that she couldn't recognize half of them.

Flossie quickly put on the coat, remembering to do the buttons up, one by one. She closed her eyes and wished and wished and wished that she could be eighteen. Once again, when she emerged, she had miraculously become Floz, a very grown-up, very smart, even rather fashionable, eighteen-year-old.

There was a sniff outside the bedroom door and Floz felt alarmed for a moment. Fergus did have a bad cold. In fact he always had a bad cold and seemed to sniff and cough his way through life. Eating with him at the table, that was the worst thing of all.

"No, it's not Fergus," thought Floz. "He wouldn't dare come into Bella's room. No one would dare to come into Bella's room. Would they . . . ?"

She opened Bella's door and there was Fido, waiting for her. He wagged his tail and looked up at her with big, moist eyes, hoping she might be about to take him for a walk.

71

Fido knew that inside the tall, smart figure of the eighteen-year-old Floz was the little, rather plumpish figure of ten-year-old Flossie, his best friend in the Teacake family, though she could be horrible to him at times.

Fido was the only person who ever recognized Floz. To everyone else in the family she appeared a stranger. She was perhaps slightly familiar, being a little bit like Bella, but then a lot of teenagers these days did look very like Bella.

It was her smell. That had not changed. That was how Fido always knew who it was.

"Sorry, Fido," said Floz. "Not now. I gotta go to work. And when you gotta go, you gotta go . . ."

"Have you any experience of shops?" asked the manageress of Flash Boutique, Fashions for the Fashionable Miss.

"Lots," said Floz, giving her head a little shake so that her long, dark hair fell over the collar of her fur coat.

"Woolworths, Marks and Spencer," said Floz. "They know me very well there. And Hamleys. I've been there many a time."

"But that's a toy shop," said the manageress. She was called Shirley and she must have been quite old, well, over thirty-five, but she was wearing a very short pink mini skirt, a tight satin polo-neck and bright blue shiny tights. Her wrists and neck and fingers were covered with gold charms and ornaments so that when she moved she jingled, like Santa Claus coming.

"I wasn't there long," said Floz. "Just half an hour. But I also worked in a hamburger restaurant. I was very good there. They said I was the best waitress they'd ever had."

Shirley wasn't sure if a hamburger waitress was the sort of person Flash Boutique needed. It was a very new shop, so she wanted to create the right impression from the beginning. The High Street wasn't particularly smart, but Shirley saw it as one of her aims to raise the tone and show the rest of the local shops how a really fashionable and modern shop should be run.

"Oh, and I did run my own hair salon for a while," said Floz. "That was fantastic. People talked about that for ages."

"Have you got any references?" asked Shirley.

"What do you think I am?" said Floz. "A map?"

She remembered that Miss Button had once given a lesson on something to do with map references.

"I mean people who can recommend you," said Shirley.

"Mrs Onions," said Floz. "She'll tell you that no one else has ever cut her hair quite like Floz."

"Well," said Shirley, thinking hard. Floz did look rather unusual in her dark fur coat and she did seem quick and confident, and running her own hair salon did show signs of real enterprise.

"I'll give you a trial for this afternoon. But you'd better work hard."

"Thanks, Miss," said Floz. "I mean Madam. I mean Shirley. I mean, thanks."

Floz wasn't quite sure how you addressed manageresses. After all, she had never worked in a shop before.

Inside, Flash Boutique was much bigger than it looked from the outside, a sort of Aladdin's cave with mirrors and special displays and flashing lights and loud music.

Shirley stayed at the front, to pounce on any customers, and then she directed them to the kind of clothes they might want—skirts, shoes, tops, under-clothes, dresses, separates.

Floz had been sent to Separates, though she wasn't quite sure what that meant.

There were two girls, one with pink hair and one with green, sitting on a couch in the Separates department, both talking loudly at the same time, both going on about their boyfriends and what they had done last night.

"Can I help you?" said Floz, going up to them. "We have some special separates in today. Freshly picked."

"You what?" said one of the girls, chewing gum.

Floz thought they might be actresses on their afternoon off. Their faces were so heavily covered in make-up that they might well have been about to go on stage.

"Would you like some separates?" said Floz. "They're all home grown."

Floz had been in many shops in her time, with her

mother of course, and was trying hard to remember what shop-keepers usually said when they were boasting about their wonderful goods. It was, though, a bit difficult to talk above the loud pop music.

"Excuse me asking," said Floz, bending down so they could hear her better. Their hair was terrific. Perhaps they might be models. "But where do you work?"

"Here, you silly cow," said the girl with the pink hair.

"Oh," said Floz. She was taken by surprise. But they both smiled. "So do I. I've been given a trial, just for this afternoon."

"Well, if you're going to work here, we don't have to," said the green-haired girl. "This place is dead anyway, but dead. I was just saying to Wayne last night, I don't know why I work here, I really don't . . ."

They quickly ignored Floz and returned to chatting to each other once again.

When customers did arrive, they very kindly explained to Floz where things were and what to do and how to do it, all the time sitting on the couch and gossiping to each other. Floz just had to ask, and they told her what to do.

It meant that quite quickly Floz began to understand how the shop worked and how to deal with customers.

Floz was having a lot of trouble with a very posh lady who didn't like any of the dresses she had insisted on trying on. They were either too long, too short, too big, too narrow, too cheap, too expensive.

"Perhaps Madam is too fat," said Floz.

"What was that?" said the posh lady.

Luckily, the sound of the music had drowned Floz's rude remark.

Floz went to the racks and got out a huge dress in a hideous green stripe. She persuaded the lady it was just what she wanted.

"It's the very latest dress. Just come from Paris," said Floz. "They didn't like it there, so we've got it."

"But is it my size?"

"Nothing's your size, dear," said Floz. "Unless it's a tent."

"What did you say, girl?" demanded the lady. She

had managed to catch a few words of what Floz had said, despite the loud music.

"I'm just a temp," said Floz. "That's what I said. You know, I work here temporarily."

Floz took the dress and led the lady into the changing cubicle. The dress was the largest size they had, but Floz knew it still wouldn't fit her.

Floz went across to the girls, still talking on the couch, and asked them where they kept the scissors. They pointed to a drawer, so Floz got them out and went back to see how the lady was getting on.

It was one of those large changing cubicles, very modern, which lots of people can use at the same time. Floz stood behind the lady, who had somehow managed to force herself into the dress, and started cutting it at the back.

"Breathe in, darling," said Floz. "You've zipped it up too far. It's not meant to go as high as that. No wonder it doesn't fit. Silly old you." Then Floz added, rather more quietly, "Silly old moo."

"Oh, that's marvellous," said the lady. "Now it fits me perfectly. I must be losing weight after all."

She stood in front of the mirror, admiring herself.

"It's *you*, Madam," said Floz. "I've never seen

anything more like you before. Luckily . . ."

"Oh, I know you assistants. You just flatter all the customers. But I do admit it does look rather charming. How does it look at the back?"

She started to turn round, but Floz stopped her just in time. She would have noticed where Floz had cut the material.

"It's best if Madam stands still," said Floz, firmly. "To get the best effect. I'll move the shop round . . ."

The woman laughed at Floz's joke. She really was very pleased with the dress.

"Oh, only one thing," said the lady. "Have you got it with short sleeves?"

"Of course, Madam," said Floz. "Anything Madam wants. Just take it off, please. I'll need to match the exact colour."

Floz took the dress into the store room and cut off the sleeves. Then she came back and handed it very carefully to Madam.

"I think you'll find this will do nicely. Perfect fit at the back. Perfect short sleeves."

With Floz's help the lady put it on.

"You're right, it's perfect," she said. "I will

definitely come to this shop again."

Shirley, the manageress, happened to be passing and heard this. She was pleased with the new assistant, though the dress being wrapped up for the customer looked somehow strange. She recognized the pattern, but not the design. How peculiar. She must be forgetting what was in her own stock.

"I would like a mini skirt," said a very tall thin lady to Floz.

Floz had been very busy and was hoping for a rest, perhaps a sit-down with the two other assistants who hadn't sold a thing so far. Floz had sold lots and was feeling a bit tired. Cutting heavy material with a pair of scissors, especially when pretending not to, can be very tiring on the wrists.

"Mini skirts are out," said Floz. "But I could sell you a Mini Bus. Our school has one which is falling to pieces . . ."

"Of course they're not out," said the customer. "I distinctly saw a lady at the front of the shop wearing one."

"That was no lady," said Floz. "That was the

Queen. But don't tell anyone. She gets *all* her dresses here."

"I'm not too tall for a mini skirt, am I?" asked the thin lady.

"Oh no, with Madam's figure," said Floz, "Madam can wear anything . . . and still look horrible."

"What was that?"

"And still look wonderful," said Floz. "Your own dress looks terrific. I like those old-fashioned long dresses."

"Thank you," said the lady, "but it's a mini skirt I want."

Floz knew there were no mini skirts in stock. She'd sold them all. She was also getting fed up with hanging around while fussy ladies got changed and unchanged and dashed back and forward into the cubicle. There must be a simpler way of selling clothes.

"You happen to be very lucky," said Floz. "We've got a new machine in today which turns dresses into mini skirts. Please close your eyes. It's a secret invention, not yet on the market. That's how the lady at the front got her mini."

The customer looked confused, but she closed her eyes and stood in her dress while Floz bent down and started cutting a huge band off the bottom. She kicked it quickly into a corner. The dress was very badly cut and there were lots of bits hanging down but Floz went to the desk and got some Sellotape to stick them up.

"Now, open your eyes. Isn't it fantastic?"

"It does look a bit strange," said the lady.

"All new fashions look a little bit strange at first," explained Floz. "I remember when the sack dress came in, some people laughed. And then hot pants. And as for ra ra skirts, in this shop, we called them ha ha skirts. Ho ho."

The lady was still a bit worried.

"As a special one-day, super promotion, we are also offering a *free* mini skirt with every one we alter," said Floz. "You are lucky. And it's only one pound."

"That's cheap," said the lady.

"All our stock is reduced today," said Floz. "They start off normal, then I reduces them." Floz burst out laughing at her own joke, but then stopped, just in time.

"What sort of mini skirts are you giving away?" asked the lady.

"By an amazing coincidence," said Floz, "we have one in the same pattern as the one you are wearing."

Floz went over into the corner, where she had kicked away the large piece of material cut from the lady's dress, and quickly picked it up and put it in a bag.

"Thank you, Madam. This is one of the neatest mini skirts you have ever seen. Madam will not be disappointed."

"Can I see it, please?" said the lady.

"Save it for when you get home, if I were you," said Floz. "Actually, it's free. No charge at all today. As I told you, everything is being reduced in this shop . . ."

Shirley decided that as Floz had made such a big success of the Separates department she should now go into shoes. That was what Floz really wanted to do most of all.

Her first customer was a woman in tweeds who said she wanted a very strong pair of shoes, to go fell-walking in.

"This is a fashion shop," said Floz. "Do you mind."

"Well, I want to look fashionable on the fells. I've spent years walking the Andes. Now I'm going to do the Lake District."

Floz looked around the shoe department, but she could see no strong boots or shoes of any sort, that was apart from the suede boots in the window. They were too good for rough walking, and anyway Floz was certainly not selling them. Floz was hoping that if she made a lot of money, she would be able to buy them for herself.

Almost all the shoes in Flash Boutique were very flimsy and light, more like slippers than walking shoes. Then Floz suddenly saw a rather large heavy shoe, with metal bits on it, lying on the floor. Someone had obviously been trying it on. Floz handed it to the woman.

"I'm not going to the moon," said the woman. "All I'm doing is Helvellyn."

"No need to swear," said Floz. "This will do you perfectly."

"Anyway, it's too big," said the woman.

"No problem," said Floz. "I can see a way of

adjusting it."

Floz had noticed some screws and cogs on the side of the shoe, presumably to make it bigger or smaller. What a brilliant idea, she thought. All shoes should be made like this. Perfect for children. As you grew bigger, the shoes grew with you.

"They are the very latest invention," said Floz. "This is the first pair to be made in the whole world. Once people see you, everyone will want them."

The woman stood up, then fell over.

"It's far too heavy," she said. "I can't walk in this."

"Don't be a silly billy," said Floz. "Your ankles are obviously too weak. And I thought you were going fell-walking. This is exactly what you want. But you'll need both shoes on to be really strong."

"Where's the other one, then?" said the woman. "I'm in a frightful hurry."

"Keep your hair on," said Floz. "You're not the boss of the whole world."

Floz went round and round the shoe department and eventually found the other large shoe. A bad-tempered-looking girl had her foot in it at the time, but Floz just grabbed it from her. She didn't realize it was still attached to the girl until Floz had dragged her half way across the shop.

"Look, love," said Floz. "I haven't time to play silly games. I'm working."

The girl was too breathless to complain. Floz untied her from the shoe and pushed her back across the floor. It was one of those very shiny tiled floors, the sort they have in Italian restaurants. The girl went shooting off like an ice-hockey puck and landed with a crash against the wall, bringing down a large pile of shoes, right on top of Shirley's head.

It was just as well that Shirley did not see the tweedy woman who was going fell-walking as she struggled out of the shop. Floz had sold her the shop's only two measuring instruments, the metal frames you put your foot in so the assistant can tell you what size shoe you need.

"I dunno," said Floz. "Some shoes are jolly difficult to sell. Not sure if I want to do this full-time . . ."

Floz then served a number of young girls, all with their mothers, mostly about ten or eleven, looking

86

for new shoes to start the new school term. Floz assured their mothers that the flimsiest, silliest shoes were perfect, recommended by the best doctors all over the world.

When one mother protested that the colours were too bright and lurid and would get dirty very quickly, Floz found a quick way of solving that problem.

She had noticed that on the counter in the shoe department they sold laces, shoe polish and spray-on dyes in different colours, for making your shoes any colour you liked.

Floz started with black, which was the colour the first mother had wanted. It took quite a while to learn how to use it and she practised in a corner, but once she perfected the paint sprays, there was no stopping her. She sprayed everyone's shoes, whether they wanted it or not: sometimes their feet and legs as well.

"Sorry about that," said Floz, when a little girl got the dye on her hair. "It's only joke paint. Comes off in seconds. No problem. But you can have the shoes for nothing. Just keep it a secret."

Soon people were leaving the shoe department

spattered in multi-coloured paints, but also clutching large parcels of shoes, most of which they had not paid for.

Shirley did not realize, of course, that Floz was letting people off and not taking the right money from them, but she was pleased to see so many people being served and going away contented.

"You've done very well today," she said to Floz. "You can start properly on Monday, if you like."

"Sorry," said Floz. "Got school on Monday. Miss Button, top Juniors . . ."

"What? You're not still at school, are you? You told me you were over eighteen."

"Oh, yeh, London School of Fashion and Design. I'm the top Junior Designer in the whole of Britain. I'm doing a degree in Action Painting."

Floz had heard Bella's friend talking about what you did at Art College, but she wasn't sure of the details.

"Well, perhaps you'll come again in your next vacation," said Shirley. "Anyway, I'll pay you now. It's nearly five o'clock and we're about to close."

"Nearly five o'clock!" Floz knew that her mother would be home any minute and would ring Carol's house if she wasn't home for supper by six.

Shirley was holding out five pounds which Floz grabbed and dashed for the door; then she rushed back again and ran to the shop window. The pink suede boots, the ones she had set her heart on, had gone.

"Oh, no," said Floz. "Someone else must have sold them. Or have they been pinched?"

Floz climbed into the window and looked around. She couldn't see the pink boots anywhere.

Then, in a far corner, lying on the floor, she noticed what looked like an almost identical pair of suede boots. They were the right size and the right shape. But they were black. She picked them up—and immediately her hand turned black. The boots were still wet with some sort of black paint.

"It must have been me," thought Floz. "When I was experimenting with that first lot of black paint. I must have sprayed some into the window by mistake."

Floz picked the boots up, and carefully closed the front window. The boots were priced at £19.99, according to the label, just like most of the shoes in the shop. Floz decided they were really only worth five pounds, so she put the money Shirley had given her into the till and wrapped up the boots for herself.

"After all," she said, running out of the shop towards home, "they were shop-soiled . . ."

The Teacakes were all sitting round the supper table when Flossie entered the kitchen.

She had managed to creep into the house without them hearing her by putting her hand through the letter box to get the key, in the secret way she was not supposed to. She had been upstairs and taken off the Magic Fur Coat and put it away safely. She was now back to being Flossie, the ten-year-old.

"Wash your hands, Flossie," said Mrs Teacake. "They're filthy. What have you been doing?"

"Finger paints, Mum," said Flossie. "Carol's got some new ones."

"And not in the kitchen sink!" said Mr Teacake as Flossie was about to put her hands under the taps.

"Sor-ree," apologized Flossie. "Keep your hair on, Dad. What's left of it . . ."

She dashed out to the wash basin under the stairs and quickly scrubbed her hands, then rushed back again. She was starving. It had been a very energetic afternoon.

"What you got on your feet, Flossie?" said Bella.

"Toes," said Flossie. "Five each side. Ain't you got any, then?"

"Don't say 'ain't'," said Mr Teacake.

"I mean those new boots, clever clogs," said Bella.

"Oh, these old things. I found them on a skip. You're not the only one, see, Bella. Then I painted them at Carol's."

"They're quite nice," said Mrs Teacake. She was standing at the kitchen sink, draining the spaghetti, waiting for Flossie so the meal could be served.

"Thanks, Mum," said Flossie. "Glad you like them. 'Cos I'm wearing them to school tomorrow. I'll keep the Clark's shoes for best. You did say I had to wear black for school . . ."

3
Flossie
at the Fête

Flossie Teacake was in the queue for school dinners. Some people stand in queues. Some people even sit in queues. And there are people who *sleep* in queues. Flossie knew that because she had seen them doing it at the Promenade Concerts. She thought that was pretty stupid. Imagine sleeping on the pavement. You had to be really stupid to do that. Or perhaps eighteen and grown up and allowed to stay out all night like her big sister Bella.

What Flossie was doing in the queue for school dinners was *leaning*. Flossie Teacake was leaning in the queue.

It had taken Flossie many months to perfect this technique, but she had now turned it into a fine art. She was able, without hardly thinking about it, to lean forward and look right round the people ahead and count with her beady eyes the exact number of pieces left in the tray of fish fingers. If she worked out that there were more people ahead of her than there were fish fingers left, then there were several things she could do.

She could shout, "Fire" and go "Ding, Ding, Ding. Everyone in the Playground."

She had done that once. In the pandemonium, Flossie had gone straight to the top of the queue while all the bemused children who had been ahead were rushing like dum dums towards the door into the playground. Afterwards, Miss Button had been very cross.

Flossie had been told off very severely and warned about crying "Wolf" ever again. Flossie wasn't sure what that meant. She thought it might be some stupid fairy story, or perhaps a parable. Or even a fable. Flossie hated all those soppy stories about the olden days. She much preferred stories about today, especially funny ones.

"You've dropped some money."

That was another trick Flossie used. It usually meant that at least three children stopped and started looking down on the floor of the dining room. Meanwhile, Flossie could jump ahead of them in the queue. But you had to make sure that you didn't do this too often to the same people. Most of the other kids in her school might be pretty stupid, apart from Flossie Teacake, or so she thought, but they weren't all *that* stupid.

But what Flossie did mostly, when she feared there might not be enough portions left of her favourite food, was very simple. She just pushed people out of the queue.

"I used to get pushed out of the queue," Flossie always told herself, fighting off any guilty feelings. "When I was in the first year, it always happened. And in the second year. And even in the third year. Now it's my turn."

It was the custom in Flossie's school for the fourth year, the top year in the Junior Department of her Primary School, all of whom were now ten years old, plus a few who were already eleven, to be served last at school dinners. That was a custom which had gone back for ages and ages and ages. For at least four years. That was as far back as Flossie could remember most things. Before that, there was a big blank. History had not yet begun.

"S'allright," said Flossie, smiling.

She had counted out that today there were easily enough fish fingers to go round. She might even get seconds, if she was quick. And the tray of chips looked ginormous. So that was all right as well.

"Yes, s'allright, Carol," said Flossie. "But I much preferred last week's *Top of the Pops*. Much better, didn't you fink, hmm?"

At the same time as Flossie had been carefully examining and calculating the fish fingers in her head, she had been outwardly carrying on a conversation with her best friend, Carol Carrot.

The two of them were standing in the queue, side by side. Apart from Flossie who was, of course, *leaning* in the queue. Carol was the one just standing.

This was what made queuing for school dinners all the more difficult. Flossie had taught herself to pretend that she was not concerned about calculating the chips or hamburgers, but just standing with her friends, idly chatting.

Sometimes, so it seemed to Flossie, a whole lifetime passed, just waiting and wondering and leaning in the dinner queue . . .

"You going to the Fête tomorrow, Flosh?" said Carol. They were now sitting at their table, stuffing the fish fingers down as quickly as possible, one eye on the serving hatch.

"S'pose so, Cash," said Flossie.

Each day they had a new name for each other, a variation on their real names. Some days they didn't use any names. Those were the days they were not talking to each other at all. At the moment, they were best friends, so that meant a great deal of talking.

"Lots of new stalls this year, Flosh," said Carol.

"I bet they'll all be boring," said Flossie. "The same old stuff."

The annual School Fête was a very big event. Hundreds and hundreds of people came and every classroom was decorated and all the playgrounds covered in activities and stalls.

Flossie was in fact looking forward to it very much. But when you get to the fourth year, top of the school, you must not appear *too* excited.

"They're having a gypsy telling fortunes," said Carol. "And there's gonna be donkey rides in the Infants' playground."

97

"Oh, you're giving rides, are you?" said Flossie. "Always knew you was a donkey."

"Oh, shurrup, you," said Carol. "Think you're so clever, Flossie Teacake. You're just a pain."

"It's you that will have the pain," said Flossie. "Giving donkey rides."

Flossie and Carol started pushing each other. They were so busy trying to get in sly pinches and thumps that they were not paying proper attention when Miss Button announced that it was now time for the fourth years to have their pudding. There had been no seconds of fish fingers after all. The dinner ladies had gone straight on to puddings.

It was chocolate cake for pudding, Flossie and Carol's favourite. Or was ice-cream their favourite? Ice-cream was so rare at school dinners that they often forgot to count that when they were bringing up to date their all-time list of best favourite school meals.

After chocolate cake, they liked apple pie or apple crumble. They also liked jelly. Their worst puddings were semolina, tapioca and prunes. Yuck.

As for main courses, fish and chips, or fish fingers and chips, were their best, followed by roast chicken, roast beef, hamburgers and then sausages.

Their worst main courses were salad, but then everyone hated salad, followed by cheese pie and then stew.

Liver would easily have made the world's worst-ever most horrible, most nasty, most awful, most yucky main course, but luckily at Flossie's school they had only had that once in living memory. Once too many, so Flossie always maintained.

Flossie and Carol jumped up, as soon as they realized puddings had started, but they found themselves at the very end of the queue.

"Oh, God," said Flossie. "Look at all those kids ahead of us. Oh, no."

"Your fault," said Carol. Whenever anything went wrong, Carol always tried to work out whose fault it was. This was one of the reasons Flossie so often hated her.

"And I know what most of those stupid little kids will do," moaned Flossie. "They'll take their share—and then they'll leave half of it."

Flossie used to do much the same, when she was in the lower years. In those far-off days, she didn't seem to have such a big appetite and she often just picked at her food. But now, as a big ten-year-old, she had developed a big appetite.

Flossie maintained she now needed to eat a lot. You had to be big and strong to beat up those fourth-year boys, such as Tommy and Billy, two boys in her class she really hated.

Tommy and Billy were in fact quite small and weedy. Flossie and Carol were much bigger than they were, without the extra help of extra helpings, but Flossie maintained they had to be prepared as any day Tommy and Billy might start their growth spurt, whatever that was. Her mother worked at a doctor's and knew about such things.

"Sorry, love," said Mrs Bunn, the chief dinner lady. "All finished."

Just as Flossie got to the counter, Mrs Bunn lifted up the empty pudding tray, almost hitting Flossie in the face, as if delighted to have finished everything off, and whisked it away behind the hatch.

"There's some bits left," said Flossie. "I saw them. Some bits of pudding left in the corner."

"Don't be greedy, child," said Mrs Bunn.

She was quite old, Mrs Bunn, but she wore very thick make-up and heavy lipstick and very tight clothes to make herself look younger. Flossie had never liked Mrs Bunn.

Flossie always tried to get served by Mrs Cabbage who usually gave Flossie a wink and sometimes double helpings, when no one was looking. Mrs Cabbage was fond of telling Flossie to "Keep up your strength, you'll need it in the race." Flossie always asked her what race, though she knew the answer. Mrs Cabbage would then say "The Human Race" and laugh so much at her own wit that she sometimes gave Flossie a third helping.

But today, of all days, when it was chocolate pudding, and Flossie had been hoping it would be Mrs Cabbage and she might even get thirds, Mrs Cabbage was off and it turned out to be horrible old Mrs Bunn.

"I bet you've just done that," said Flossie. "Keeping the pudding for yourself . . ."

"I'll report you to the Headmistress," said Mrs Bunn.

"Don't care," said Flossie.

"Some of these fourth years are getting far too lippy, if you ask me."

"Nobody asked you," said Flossie, turning away.

She was almost in tears, but fourth-year girls don't cry. "It's just not fair!"

Flossie and Carol were leaning against the lavatory walls in the playground. Flossie had her angriest face on and looked so furious that Carol was scared to talk to her.

Suddenly, Flossie ran forward and gave a huge kick. Carol jumped out of the way, thinking Flossie was going to take her anger out on her, but all Flossie was doing was kicking the boys' football.

They were in the Junior playground and in the Junior playground the boys were allowed to play football. That was also unfair, as it ruined the playground for the girls' games, but that was a minor unfairness, compared with some unfairnesses Flossie could mention.

"Serves you right," said Flossie, as Billy and Tommy came rushing up.

Flossie's kick had been so hard and furious that it had sent the football high over the wire fence and out into the main road. The boys were not allowed to go out in the road and retrieve the ball. It was dangerous.

"You've ruined our game," said Billy.

"Hard luck," said Flossie. "I don't care."

"Just 'cos you didn't get no pudding," said Tommy, laughing at her.

Oh, God, thought Flossie. The whole school must know about it by now. She really hated that Mrs Bunn.

"You're too fat anyway," said Billy.

"Do you want to get thumped?" said Flossie.

She glared hard at Billy, then she ran forward, trying to kick him, but he was too quick. Although he was smaller and weedier than Flossie, he could run like a whippet. She chased him twice round the playground, scattering the younger children as she ran, without even getting near him.

Then she sat down again beside Carol, tired and exhausted now, and still as furious as ever.

"I've got a plan," said Flossie. "Just listen . . ."

The Headmistress, Miss Henn, was on the telephone. Flossie and Carol could hear her discussing something to do with amplifiers and loud speakers for the Fête.

They were keeping an eye out for the School Secretary whose office was next door to the Head-mistress's. You were supposed to go to her office first, if you wanted to see the Head, but Flossie had decided not to.

"Shouldn't we tell the Secretary?" said Carol.

"This is too important," said Flossie. "She'll just tell us to come back on Monday. I know her."

At last, they could hear Miss Henn hanging up the telephone. Flossie gave Carol a push against the door. Just a little push, to help her forward, to encourage her to knock at the door. Flossie had decided that Carol would be the one who knocked at the Head's door. Carol thought the push was too hard, in fact far too hard, more a thump than a gentle push, so she pushed Flossie back.

As they pushed and argued, Miss Henn opened the door and they both fell into the Head's office.

Flossie had only been in the Head's office twice before. Once when she took a late register and once in the first year when she got a star for good work. She had not had any stars for good work recently. But, as Flossie now thought, stars were pretty stupid.

The Headmistress's office smelled strange to Flossie; a smell she could not quite identify, a mixture of detergent, as if in a hospital, mixed with smoke, like the top of a bus.

"Yes, can I help you two girls?" said Miss Henn, going back to her desk and waving them to sit down.

"We're a diputation," began Flossie. "We've been sent, you see, 'cos, we're a diputation . . ."

"You mean deputation," said Miss Henn. "What exactly is the problem?"

"Nothing, Miss," said Carol.

Flossie gave her a quick punch.

"It's Flossie," said Carol. "She's a problem, I mean she's got a problem . . ."

"Come on now girls, I have got a lot of important phone calls to make and tomorrow is a very busy day, for all of us . . ."

As she spoke the phone rang and she picked it up, although first of all she said, "Excuse me" to Flossie and Carol. She was at least polite to them, not like some people Flossie knew, such as those people in her own family, such as those people called Bella and Fergus.

Flossie was not sure if they were meant to leave the room or not. If they did, the Secretary might see them and they would never get in again.

"Oh, that is *too* much," said Miss Henn. "You might have told us earlier . . ."

Flossie could hear a woman's voice on the line, though rather indistinct, saying that she was sorry, but she had flu. She had tried to get someone else to take her place, but good Fortune Tellers were hard to find these days.

"What a bore," said Miss Henn, hanging up the phone. "Madame Zara has now let us down. That's the last straw. Now, quickly, girls, what is it you want to tell me?"

"Well, Miss," said Flossie, deciding to get it over with quickly. "We all fink . . ."

"We all think," said Miss Henn.

"We all think, in our class, that it's not fair that fourth years always get served last and today there was no pudding left and it's not fair and why can't the third years be last for a change 'cos we need our food more than they do and anyway we've been sent to say this to you as it's not fair, see, Miss, only . . ."

"I see," said Miss Henn. "So that's it. Hmm . . ."

"Yeh, well," said Carol, very impressed by Flossie's long speech. "We don't want to have no strike, do we, Miss?"

Flossie had told Carol not to say this. It would only be a last resort, threatening to down tools and pencils and go on strike. First of all you always had to have consultations, with a deputation putting the workers' case. Flossie had learned all this from her father. Now Carol had ruined everything.

"Oh, I'm sure it won't come to that," said Miss Henn. "You've put your case very eloquently."

"Fanks," said Flossie. Miss Henn was too busy thinking to correct her this time.

"Now, I want you to report back to the whole fourth year—you did say you represent them all, that they elected you to come here?"

Flossie nodded her head. So did Carol, when she saw Flossie's nod.

"Right, well tell them I will consider your points and deliberate over the weekend. I will then give my considered view on Monday. Please close the door when you go out . . ."

It was just a few minutes before two o'clock and the queue to get into the School Fête was a good hundred metres down the main road. There were a lot of old ladies carrying rather large carrier bags. There were also quite a few young ladies, carrying even larger bags. Bella Teacake was one of the younger ladies, hoping for a good haul from the second-hand clothes stall. That was where she got all her best clothes.

Two parents were on the gate, waiting to open up and take the ten p admission charges. Children and unemployed and Old Age Pensioners were of course half-price. They had a pile of change in front of them on a desk, knowing that there would be a lot of people without the correct money.

At one minute to two o'clock, as the two parents were about to open the main gates and let in the hordes, a strange-looking young lady in a fur coat and a mass of silk scarves which flowed behind her in the wind, covering most of her hair and her shoulders, rushed to the top of the queue.

She had very brown skin, unnaturally brown skin, almost as if she had been putting on dark brown make-up with a trowel. This was almost true. Floz had in fact used a kitchen knife to apply Bella's make-up. It was all she could find.

Bella had of course left early, to get in the queue,

and so had Mr and Mrs Teacake. They were slightly further down the queue. Like all good parents, they never missed a School Fête. Fergus was not in the queue, or anywhere near the school. It was Saturday afternoon. He had set off hours ago to go and watch Spurs.

So, just for once Flossie had had the house to herself, time to step into her Magic Fur Coat, into her eighteen-year-old body, and become eighteen-year-old Floz. But it had been a bit of a rush, putting on the extra touches. This time, it was her appearance as well as her age which had to look exactly right . . .

"Excuse me," said Floz, flashing what she thought was a mysterious gypsy smile. "I am Madame Flozo."

"Pardon?"

"I'm working here today," said Floz. "Indeed to goodness. Actually, don't you know, what what. Och aye."

Floz was not quite sure what accent gypsies used.

"What was that?" said the parent in charge, who happened to be Mrs Carrot, Carol's mother. She looked at Floz, wondering where she had seen her face before, or someone very much like her.

"Madame Flozo," said Floz. "I'm your Fortune Teller. It's on the programme. Go on, have a look."

"Oh, I'm terribly sorry," said Mrs Carrot. "I quite forgot. Of course you are. You're one of the stars of the Fête. Very sorry. Come straight in, quick, before we open."

"Thanks awfully," said Floz, deciding perhaps a posh accent would be suitable. "You didn't want me to put a spell on you, did you, ha ha ha . . ."

"Certainly not," said Mrs Carrot. "Should I take you to your place? Let me see, you're in Room H, Miss Button's room. I'll take you there. This school can be very confusing."

"No, no," said Floz. "I know exactly where it is. Been there hundreds of times, ain't I."

For a moment, Floz had forgotten her gypsy accent.

"I mean," said Floz, recovering quickly, "I've been there hundreds of times, in my crystal ball . . ."

Madame Flozo was proving an enormous success.

She seemed to be able to reveal personal details about every single person who came into her tent. There was quickly a huge queue waiting to get into Room H and as people stood there, they swopped stories about other people who had already had their fortunes told. They all agreed it was uncanny how much Madame Flozo could guess about a person just by examining their hands.

Her tent was in the corner of the classroom, erected by Miss Button out of an old wigwam left over from the nursery. She had provided a little oil lamp for the Fortune Teller, and had switched the classroom lights off at the main switch. Everyone coming into Room H appeared at first to be coming into the dark. It therefore took them a while to focus on Madame Flozo and her crystal ball.

It was in fact a globe of the world. Floz had taken it from Miss Button's store cupboard and covered it with with red tissue paper. She had also brought a pack of cards with her, belonging to Fergus, just in case.

Floz's eyes had soon got completely used to the half light and she knew everyone by sight the minute they entered her tent: not only their names but their favourite pudding, their worst meal, their best football team, how many sisters they had, how many brothers, the names of their pets, who was good at maths, where they went for their last holiday and how they got that nasty cut on the back of their left hand. It truly was amazing, so everyone thought. How could she possibly do it? It could only be magic.

"I think," said Madame Flozo, bending down and examining a lady's hand very carefully, "let me see, I think you must work with something to do with food. You're not a school dinner lady, are you, by any chance?"

"That's absolutely amazing," said Mrs Bunn.

And with that, Mrs Bunn appeared to fall over. Floz jumped up in alarm. Had Mrs Bunn fainted in alarm or astonishment? Floz didn't want that sort of thing to happen, not before she had properly begun . . .

"Sorry about that, dear," said Mrs Bunn. "I caught my foot in a bit of your tent. Ooh, I do like having me fortune told. Now, would you like to do my other hand?"

Mrs Bunn held out her left hand and Floz studied

it carefully. She didn't want to rush things this time. Having looked at it for several minutes, and not seen very much, apart from a lot of old lines, she decided to give it a sniff, the way Fido did when he was being friendly.

"Ooh, that tickles," said Mrs Bunn.

"That's the magic starting to work," said Floz. "Now, I am beginning to detect a slight trace of, let me see, what is it?"

Floz gave the hand another quick sniff.

"Chocolate pudding?" asked Floz. "Did you serve chocolate pudding yesterday?"

"You're absolutely right," exclaimed Mrs Bunn.

"Madame Flozo is always right. Never forget that," said Floz.

"I suppose the smell might have helped," said Mrs Bunn, realizing she must have given away a strong clue. "All the same, I had thought I had washed my hands terribly carefully."

"You can never be too careful," said Floz, "not when serving school dinners."

"I didn't spill anything, honest, it wasn't me. It was Ivy, she's new and always dropping things."

"So that's why you ran out of chocolate pudding

yesterday," said Floz.

"Yes, it was, but it wasn't my fault," said Mrs Bunn. Then she paused. "Gawd, you're a bleeding marvel. How did you know we ran out? You couldn't smell that, could you? Gawd, I'm getting scared in here . . ."

"Don't worry, Mrs Bunn," said Floz. She immediately regretted using Mrs Bunn's name. It would be just too clever, even for the world's best Fortune Teller, to know that, especially with such an unusual name. But Mrs Bunn had not noticed the use of her name.

"Don't tell me any bad things," said Mrs Bunn. "I don't want to know no bad things."

"You are probably not aware of the bad things you did yesterday," said Floz. "Was there not some poor child at the end of the queue who ended up with no chocolate pudding whatsoever?"

"Wasn't my fault . . ."

"But Mrs Bunn, you are the chief dinner lady. In future, I advise you to take great care. If in doubt, always make sure there is something left for the fourth years, especially that poor little girl at the end of the queue."

"Oh, she's not so poor, or little," began Mrs Bunn.

"What was that?" said Floz sternly. "I can now see some dark shadows in this crystal ball, Mrs Bunn. Do you want me to tell you what is in store for you personally . . ."

"No, no, please, no."

"Then if you are a *good* dinner lady, the shadows will go away. Madame Flozo can see into the future. Madame Flozo is always . . ."

"Thanks very much, Madame," said Mrs Bunn, "I'll have to go now. I promise to do what you say."

And she ran out of Room H, down the corridor, past the dining hall, into the playground, out into the main road, and all the way home . . .

"These hands are filthy," said Floz very severely. "Go away and wash them at once. I will not have such disgusting habits in my tent."

Tommy and Billy walked sheepishly out of the tent and across the classroom to the sink in Miss Button's store room. While they were away, Floz wrote with a very faint pencil the initials FT on the tissue paper on top of the globe.

"That's better," said Floz when they returned and meekly held out their hands for her inspection.

"I should really give you a consultation one by one, but seeing as how you are both *very* little boys, with *very* little flesh on you," said Floz, giving them both a sharp pinch, "and probably very little sense, I'll see you both together and allow you two for the price of one."

"Thanks, Miss," said Tommy.

"I am not a Miss," shouted Floz, so suddenly they both jumped. "I am Madame Flozo. On your knees, both of you."

They both fell to their knees.

"That's better. Now lick my shoes. More. That means you as well, Billy. Oh, yes, I know both your names, and your number, and your cucumber. So don't try any tricks with me. Or else . . ."

Floz put on her deepest, most menacing gypsy voice.

"Right, you can now get up. What questions do you want answered?"

"Everyfink, Miss," said Tommy.

"Who will win the F.A. Cup this year?" said Floz. "What you are getting for your birthday present? That sort of fing? I mean, thing? Yes, hmm?"

"Yes, please, Madame . . ." they both said loudly together.

"The answer is No! I will not. I don't do silly, selfish, stupid, trivial, boyish things like that. I foretell the real and important future. And it is not always very reassuring. Do you understand? Are you scared? Do you want to leave now? Come on boy, don't stutter."

"I'm no-ot scared," said Tommy.

"I am," said Billy, but Tommy kicked him to stop him shaking.

"Right, I want both of you to lay your hands flat on this magic crystal ball. That's it. Now look into my eyes. Can you feel the blood throbbing through your fingers?"

"Yeh," said Tommy.

"I can feel my pulses," said Billy.

"Exactly," said Floz. "The magic is working, reaching the pulses other magics can't. I'll count to ten and say the magic words. Flozo ozo, ozo flozo."

"My hands are shaking," said Tommy.

"Right," said Floz, "take your hands away. If the magic has worked, the crystal ball will have written down some initials on the exact spot where your fingers were lying. Can you read them, Tommy?"

"No, Miss. I mean no, Madame."

"Can you read anything?" said Floz. "Can you do joined-up writing yet? What about you, Billy?"

Floz moved her oil lamp a little nearer so that Billy could see the two letters on the tissue paper.

"It looks like an E," stuttered Tommy. "And a T. ET! Oh, no!"

"I'm going," said Billy. They both turned to run away.

"I don't want no ET chasing me," said Tommy. "That film was really scary . . ."

"Come back here, you silly boys," commanded Floz. "You haven't read it properly. Look, that's not an E."

"Oh, yeh," said Billy. "It's an F. FT it says."

"Exactly," said Floz. "Those are the initials of the person who in the future is going to be the most influential person in your life."

"I don't know anyone called FT, do you, Billy?" said Tommy.

"No, I don't know, either, Miss."

"Well, just think, very slowly. It is very important for both of you. You must always be extra kind and helpful whenever you deal with this person."

"Isn't that the name of a newspaper?" said Tommy. "One of them posh papers, sort of pink. I fink. When I help my brother with his paper round, he has to deliver a few F.T.'s . . ."

"No, not *Financial Times*," said Floz. "This is a person, a real-life human being. Come on, think of people you know whose names begin with the letter F."

They both looked blank. Eventually Tommy spoke.

"I know a big boy called Fergus, well, sort of know him. I know his little sister better. She's horrible. Is it Fergus, Miss?"

"No," said Floz. She was beginning to become

impatient with their stupidity. "Who said it was a boy? It might be a girl, even a little girl, of your age . . ."

"We don't know no girls, Miss," said Billy. "We don't play with no girls."

"Then perhaps you had better, in the future," said Floz. "It is very important that you treat any girl with the initials FT in an extra-special way from now on. Any girl called FT who might happen, for example, to be in your class . . ."

Floz paused. They both still looked completely vacant.

"Oh, get out," said Floz. "You are just too stupid."

Tommy and Billy left the tent and went slowly across to the classroom door. Just as they were leaving, Tommy clutched hold of Billy's hand.

"I've gorrit. Flossie . . ."

"Next please," said Floz, in her best gypsy voice.

It was Miss Henn, the Headmistress. Floz's first reaction was to hide under the flaps of the tent, but they were pinned to the floor. Then she tried to dodge into the store room, but Miss Henn was already inside the tent before she could get out.

"Gosh, this is fun," said Miss Henn. "Jolly good of you to turn up, Madame Flozo. I presume Madame Zara told you about us. I was very worried we'd end up with nobody."

"We Fortune Tellers stick together," said Floz. "One for all, all for one."

"What fun. That sounds like The Three Musketeers."

"Yes," said Floz. "We all go there for our holidays."

"What?" said Miss Henn. "Oh, jolly funny. Anyway, I hear you've been a bit of a success. Everyone is talking about you and your marvellous feats of clairvoyancing."

"I haven't done her yet," said Floz. "I've only done one Claire, Claire Windmill in Miss Button's class."

"Jolly good," said Miss Henn. "Ha ha ha. You must be exhausted, with all this *magic* you have been working."

Miss Henn gave Floz a huge wink, just to let her know that she personally did not believe in palm reading or fortune telling. Or was it because she realized who Madame Flozo was? For a moment, Floz was not sure.

"I wouldn't do that, if I were you," said Floz. "Not with contact lenses."

"How did you know?" said Miss Henn. "That's awfully good."

Miss Henn had given a talk about her new contact lenses in Assembly only the other week, which is how everyone in the school knew about them.

"But I see that your husband hasn't got them yet," said Floz, gazing at her globe. "Is he too scared? He should have them; he really can't drive properly. One day the police will get him. In fact this afternoon I've had one policeman, Carol Carrot's father, he's a sergeant, CID, you know, and he was telling me . . ."

This string of inside information was just too much for Miss Henn. She looked utterly amazed.

"How on earth did you know all that?"

"I told you. I know everything about this school. I even know you had important visitors after school yesterday."

"You know more than I do, then," said Miss

Henn. "I saw nobody yesterday."

"Nobody?" asked Floz.

"Well, Mr Peacock, the Inspector, was due to come, but he cancelled. Two parents said they wanted to see me, but they never appeared."

"Was that all?"

"Oh, I did talk in the corridor to the caretaker, but that was not important. No, I'm afraid you are wrong this time, Madame Flozo. I had no visitors in my office after school yesterday."

"Are you sure? Put your hands on this crystal ball and gaze into my eyes and think very, very carefully. Now, can you see any writing on the paper, any letters perhaps? Here, I'll help you with my lamp."

"C-I-," said Miss Henn, slowly spelling out the letters.

"Are you sure you've got your contact lenses in, Miss?" said Floz. "I mean Miss Henn, Madame Henn."

"Oh, that's better. It looks like FT. That's it, FT. But it means nothing to me. In don't know anybody called FT. I did have an old friend called Florence, but she died last year."

"This could be a pupil, perhaps someone in your

124

top year. Did you see any pupils yesterday after school?"

"Oh, I didn't know you meant the *children*. I thought you meant real visitors."

"Children can be important, you know," said Floz.

"Of course, Flossie and Carol. They came in a deputation. It was terribly funny, they wanted me to . . ."

"No, don't tell me," said Floz, holding up her hands. "I don't want you to tell me any of your secrets. I can find out all the secrets I want to find out, all on my own, thank you very much. I don't listen to gossip or people who tell stories about other people . . ."

For a moment, Miss Henn looked rather guilty, thinking over all the things she had been told confidentially, off the record, just for her ears only, on the QT, in the last two days.

"All that my crystal ball wants to tell you," said Floz, "is to be very careful how you handle those two young girls. It is vital you make the right decision. They are not to be treated lightly. This is a serious matter. Whatever it is they came to complain about—and I don't know what it is—then they were in the right."

"Oh, exactly," said Miss Henn. "I had been thinking that myself. It was rather unfair the way . . ."

"No, no," said Floz. "I don't want to hear any more. As you go out, please call in the next person, will you . . ."

Flossie and Carol were sitting at the dinner table eating their third helping of ice-cream. It was Monday lunch time and ice-cream had suddenly appeared on the menu.

Mrs Bunn came over and asked them, very politely, if they would like fourths. She had arranged the ice-cream, so she said, especially for them.

"Yeh, why not," said Flossie. "Just a little. If you're forcing us. And could you please take these dirty plates away."

It had been fish and chips for the main course, Flossie's favourite, and she had had double helpings. It was all very strange. Fish and chips were usually on a Friday, not a Monday, in Flossie's school. Then there was the fact that Mrs Bunn had actually come to their table to help them. That had never happened before. Probably never would again. So Flossie and Carol were making the most of it.

"Isn't it nice to be served first for a change?" said Carol.

"Yeh, but it will be our turn to be last in another four weeks," said Flossie.

"Oh, Flossie, don't be greedy," said Carol. "Miss Henn said that from now on every year will take a week each to be served first. That's only fair."

"It could be fairer-er," said Flossie. "We should have lots of privileges, being fourth years. I think we should be first *all* the time. Perhaps we should have another deputation."

"You're just joking, aren't you, Flossie?" said Carol giving her a friendly push.

"Now I'm choking," said Flossie, laughing. "Actually, I feel a bit sick. I think I've had too much ice-cream."

"I'll finish yours then, Flosh," said Carol, grabbing Flossie's plate.

Flossie smiled and leaned back on her chair, right back on two legs, the way Miss Button had told them never to do.

"Isn't it nice to watch other people standing in the queue?" said Flossie.

"*Leaning* in the queue," said Carol. "Look at those third years. Greedy Pigs. I hate people who do that in the queue, don't you, Flossie . . . ?"

"Disgusting," said Flossie. "They think nobody can see them doing it . . ."